Emily

the Rain Forest Monkey

Save The Rainforest
Best Wishes
Nancy Szelnik

Emily

the Rain Forest Monkey

Written by Nancy Skolnik and daughter, Ashley Skolnik

Illustrated by Linda Buschke

Published by Skolnik Publishing
Petaluma, California

Emily, the Rain Forest Monkey

Copyright 1997 by Nancy & Ashley Skolnik

ISBN 1-56550-077-6

Library of Congress Catalog Card No. 96-61256

Illustrated by Linda Buschke
Designed by H. Robert Brekke

Printed in Hong Kong

Skolnik Publishing
707-763-5571

This story is dedicated not to any one person but to every animal and every environment that once was.

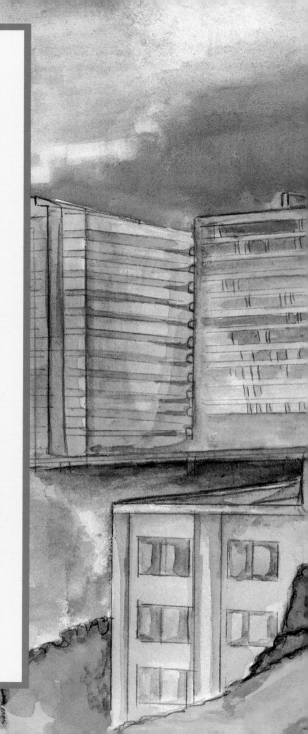

Hi! My name is Sarah Bentley. I am ten years old, and I have always had a special love for animals and the wonders of the rain forests.

My dad, Henry Bentley, works as a news reporter at a TV station. During the summer, my dad takes me to work with him, and I get to watch all the exciting things that happen at the TV station.

One day, while I was at the station, I was watching some TV screens about what is happening in the Brazilian rain forests. Trees are being cut down for lumber to build roads, mines, and dams. Many areas are being cleared and burned for raising cattle and farming. My dad was asked to travel to the Brazilian rain forest to make a news report for his station.

The trees breathe carbon dioxide and give off oxygen, which we all need to breathe. When the trees are gone, the topsoil, which nourishes plants, is washed away in the rain.

Many diseases are treated with medicine made from plants that grow only in the rain forest. These plants and many animals depend on the rain forest for survival.

The pictures of the forests being destroyed made me worry about all the plants and animals living there.

"Daddy, could I please go to the rain forest?"

"Well, Sarah, Brazil is a long trip for a little girl."

"I promise to be very good. Please, Daddy? Please, please, please?"

I couldn't believe it when he said yes!

When our plane landed in Brazil, we had to rush to catch a small helicopter that would fly us into a rain forest. It was rainy and hot—it's usually between 70 and 90º Fahrenheit there, and it rains 6 to 30 feet or more each year.

To get to our campground, we walked through miles of tropical jungle. I saw colorful birds and beautiful butterflies. Tree frogs and lizards appeared and then blended into the trees. In the distance, furry animals were running and jumping. High up in the tree canopy, monkeys were swinging and chattering.

But when we arrived at camp, the air was thick with smoke from trees burning in the distance. I could hear the chain saws cutting down trees. The smoke stung my eyes. It was hard to breathe.

The next morning, while hiking, I saw a mother monkey gathering berries and feeding them to her babies. A little dark-haired baby monkey was lagging behind. I was worried that the tree where the monkeys lived would soon be cut down and burned.

As I walked, I felt something behind me. It was the baby monkey! I told her to go home, but she followed me back to camp. I was afraid she would never find her mother again, and I decided to take care of her myself. She drank milk from my water bottle and slept in my sleeping bag every night. I named her Emily.

I knew I couldn't take Emily home with me, but I couldn't leave her all alone with no one to take care of her. My daddy knew one of the government officials. We got special permission to take Emily home with us. Emily fit perfectly inside my backpack. She was so tiny that the flight attendant let her fly with me on the plane. During the flight, she ate peanuts.

When we got home, I took Emily to my room. I put one of my little sister's diapers on her and cut a hole in it for her tail. I then fixed her a bottle of warm milk. At night I could feel her furry, cozy body cuddling against my flannel pj's. I knew she needed me.

Emily and I had so much fun together! We went to the park and had picnics in the trees. One day I took her to the grocery store, and she felt right at home. In the produce department, she went wild. She jumped out of the cart and scampered around on the fruit and started eating. The store manager frowned and told us we would have to leave because animals weren't allowed in the store.

But after a while, I noticed Emily's eyes looked sad. She was also sleeping an awful lot, so I took her to see our veterinarian, Dr. Rowe. He said I must tell my mom and dad about Emily's condition. She needed to be in tropical weather and be kept warm and eat special foods. Dr. Rowe gave me some medicine for her and said that with a lot of love, she might be okay. I cried all the way home. I was afraid she might die, and it would be all my fault for not knowing just how to care for her.

When I got home, I wrapped Emily in my flannel pj's and held her in my arms to keep her warm. I knew I had to tell my mom and dad about Emily's illness. But what if they decided to send her back to Brazil? What if she died because no one was there to take care of her? Her home was probably already destroyed by the fires.

Then I had an idea. "Maybe Emily could help us save the rain forests!"
When I finally told my mom and dad about Emily and my idea, they
were concerned, but agreed that my idea was better than sending
Emily back to Brazil.

he next morning Emily and I went down to the TV station and appeared on the news show with my dad. I talked about Emily's home being burned down and about all the special animals and plants that live in the rain forest. I told them about what the destruction was doing to the air.

People from all over called in and said they wanted to know where to donate money to help save Emily's home. Other TV stations invited us to appear on their programs, and teachers invited us into their classrooms.

Emily has made a difference. Now many people are working to save the rain forests of the world. Sometimes while she lies asleep next to me, I wonder if she dreams of her life in Brazil. I am sad that Emily lost her home and family. But I am glad that with help from me and my dad, Emily can make people realize how important the rain forest is to people and environments all over the world.

I love Emily dearly, and I hope that she and I can teach people that she was meant to live in the rain forest. For now she seems happy to be part of our family, but I know that someday she will want a rain forest family of her own.

Jon Provost

Former child actor Jon Provost has been concerned about the welfare of animals all his life. Now a family man with two children living in Santa Rosa, California, Jon is known to us all as Timmy, star of the Lassie series. His endorsement of *Emily, the Rain Forest Monkey* is a sincere attempt to encourage both children and adults that we cannot take the wonders of our earth for granted.

Jon has earned a nationwide reputation as a philanthropist, giving his time to a wide assortment of causes, including children's hospitals, humane societies, and, closest to his heart, Canine Companions for Independence, on whose Board of Governors he currently serves. In 1986, the Motion Picture Council presented him with its award for Outstanding Contribution as a humanitarian for his dedication in helping the physically challenged. In 1989, Jon and his TV mom, June Lockhart, served as national spokespersons for Snuggles' Back to School Safety Child-Savers Program. More recently, he received the Lifetime Achievement Award from the Youth In Film Association for his continuing efforts with the Easter Seals Telethon and the Citizens Advisory Committee to the American Police Hall of Fame. He has also received a Genesis Award for Outstanding Television in a Family Series for a script he wrote focusing on the inhumane treatment of research animals.